This edition published by Parragon in 2009
Parragon
Queen Street House
4 Queen Street
Bath BA1 1HE, UK

Copyright © 2009 Disney Enterprises, Inc. and Pixar.

ISBN 978-1-4075-8183-5

Printed in China

Disney · PIXAR

FINDING
NEMO

PaRragon

Bath · New York · Singapore · Hong Kong · Cologne · Delhi · Melbourne

Marlin was a clownfish – but that didn't mean he had to find life funny. All he did was worry about his little son, Nemo, who had one weak fin. Marlin had lost the rest of his family to a big bad barracuda when Nemo was just an egg. He was determined that no harm would ever befall his only son.

Nemo was a fish full of fun who was looking forward to
starting school and making friends.
But Marlin didn't even like him going outside
their home.

"What's the one thing we have to remember about the
ocean?" he asked little Nemo sternly.

"It's not safe," Nemo sighed.

On the first day of school, all the kids went on an outing to the edge of the reef. Nemo had made some new friends and, together, they sneaked off daring each other to swim out into the open sea. Nemo was nervous and didn't venture very far, but it was way too far for Marlin, who was hovering nearby.

"You think you can do these things, but you just can't, Nemo!" he yelled, rushing over.

Defiantly, Nemo decided to prove him wrong. While his dad was distracted, the little fish swam out, towards a boat anchored overhead.

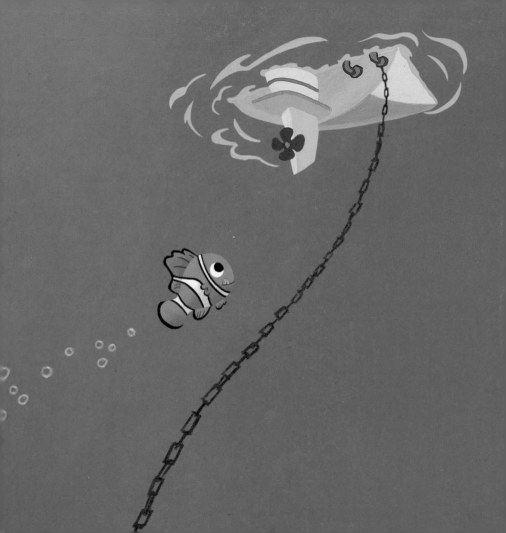

Brave Nemo had made it all the way to the boat when disaster struck – a diver grabbed him!

"Daddy, help me!" yelled Nemo as he was scooped up in a net.

"Coming, Nemo!" cried a distraught Marlin. There was nothing he wouldn't do to save his precious son.

But another diver saw him and took a photo!

Blinded by the flash for precious seconds, Marlin couldn't catch up with the disappearing divers. The boat took off so fast that a diver's mask fell overboard.

A beautiful Regal Tang Fish called Dory offered to help Marlin find Nemo, but unfortunately, she had a short-term memory problem.

"I forget things almost instantly," she explained, and promptly forgot who Marlin was.

Marlin turned to head off – and came face to face with a shark!

The shark was called Bruce. He was trying to turn vegetarian! The big bruiser wanted the fish to meet his like-minded buddies so they could prove their motto: 'Fish are friends, not food!'

Dory, as enthusiastic as she was forgetful, thought the whole thing was a great idea. Marlin – who was totally terrified – did not!

The 'self-help' sharks held their meetings in a wrecked
submarine. The meeting began.

"It has been three weeks since my last fish," Bruce told his
friends proudly.

Then Marlin spotted the mask worn by the diver who had taken
Nemo! Dory wanted to show it to the sharks but Marlin didn't.
As the two scuffled over the mask, Dory bumped her nose. It
bled a little – and Bruce got a craving for a fish dinner!

"Just a bite!" begged Bruce. His friends tried to stop him eating up Marlin and Dory but Bruce was determined! A scary skirmish ensued before the plucky fish were able to get away with the mask in tow. But Dory accidentally dropped the mask into a deep ocean trench.

When they swam down after it, the two friends discovered a scary anglerfish just waiting to pounce! Its glowing antenna was the only light this far down in the ocean.

While Marlin fought the fish, the light revealed an address on the diver's mask. Luckily, Dory remembered she could understand 'human'!

'42 Wallaby Way, Sydney, Australia," she read.

Using the mask to trap the anglerfish against a rock, Marlin and Dory set off for Sydney with new hope of finding Nemo.

Meanwhile, Nemo found himself the latest catch in a dentist's fish tank in Sydney, where he met Bubbles, Peach, Jacques, Bloat, Deb, Gurgle – and their tough-guy leader, Gill.

Poor Nemo soon discovered how small the tank was. He could hardly swim any distance without hitting the sides. Even worse Nemo heard he was to be given to the dentist's niece, a ghastly girl named Darla.

"She's a fish-killer," whispered Peach.

Later that night, the friends in the tank asked Nemo to join their gang. "If," Bloat whispered, "you are able to swim through THE RING OF FIRE!" It sounded scary, but really it was just a circle of bubbles. Nemo bravely made it through – and into the gang's hearts.

"We're gonna help him escape," Gill told his fishy friends.

Back in the ocean, Marlin and Dory were in trouble too. They had swum into a jellyfish forest and got stung. Luckily they escaped and some sea turtles gave them a ride.

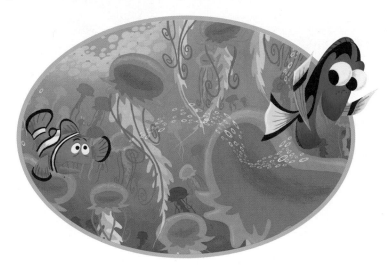

One of the little turtles did lots of daring tricks, but his father, Crush, didn't mind. He trusted his children to know their limits "How do you know they're ready?" asked Marlin. "When they know, you'll know," Crush replied.
As Marlin got closer to Sydney, tales of his adventures were spreading far and wide.

Nigel, a friendly pelican who knew the Tank Gang, eventually heard the stories and rushed to tell Nemo the incredible news.

"Your dad's been fightin' the entire ocean looking for you!" he squawked in excitement.

Nemo was amazed. He loved his dad, but had always thought him a bit of a scaredy-fish. The idea that he was battling his way to Sydney filled the little fish with pride – and new hope of returning to his ocean home.

The Tank Gang had tried and failed to escape before, but this time Nemo was determined. Bravely, he managed to jam the tank's cleaning filter with a pebble.

The water inside the tank became green and filthy. Surely the dentist would have to take out the fish to clean the tank? This would mean he would have to put them in little plastic bags. Then maybe, somehow, they might just be able to make their escape.

Back in the ocean, Marlin and Dory said goodbye to the turtles, but were soon in trouble again – with a whale! The gigantic creature scooped them into his massive mouth.

"I have to get out! I have to find my son!" Marlin wailed. "I promised I'd never let anything happen to him."

"You can't never let *anything* happen to him," Dory argued. "Then *nothing* would ever happen to him. That's not much fun."

Luckily the whale was only giving the two brave fish a lift. Soon they were squirted out of his blowhole – right into Sydney harbour!

The two friends searched for the boat that had taken Nemo, almost being eaten by Gerald the pelican. Luckily, Nigel found them just in time!

"Hop inside my mouth if you want to live," he whispered to Marlin and Dory.
Scooping them up, Nigel flew over towards the dentist's surgery.

Inside, the Tank Gang had hit trouble. The dentist had cleaned their water with a fancy new filter – while they were still in the tank! The escape plan was ruined.

"What do we do when the little brat gets here?" worried Bloat.

"I'm thinking," said Gill, a little put out that his brilliant plan hadn't worked.

But it was too late. Despite their efforts to save him, Nemo was lifted out of the tank and plopped into a bag.

Darla had arrived.

Suddenly, Nigel stumbled through the window with Marlin and Dory. The dentist quickly shooed him away, but dropped Nemo as he did so. The bag burst open!

"I get a fishy!" squealed Darla as she reached out to grab him.
But true friends are there for you whatever the risks.

Using all his strength, Gill leaped from the tank and distracted Darla, making her scream.
"Tell your dad I said hi!" Gill yelled as he managed to catapult the startled Nemo right down the sink.

Back in the tank, he reassured his friends. "Don't worry. All drains lead to the ocean."

Nigel flew back to the harbour and dropped a desolate Marlin and Dory back in the water. Marlin thought he had lost Nemo and swam sadly off. But then Nemo found Dory, and together they swam after Marlin as fast as Nemo's little fin would let them.

There was a joyful reunion, and now Marlin and Nemo both knew that life was an adventure to be lived to the full – together, and with the help of good friends.

Meanwhile, the Tank Gang were having an adventure of their own. They'd finally made their escape . . . and now they just had to get out of the bags!